Dedicated in loving memory to
Auntie Janice who always filled
our hearts with love

x

Teddy Christmas © 2017 by Allan Plenderleith
For more books by Allan visit allanplenderleith.com

First published in 2017
by
Ravette Publishing Limited
PO Box 876, Horsham, West Sussex RH12 9GH

ISBN: 978-1-84161-402-1

Printed and bound in India by Replika Press Pvt. Ltd.

# Teddy Christmas

## by Allan Plenderleith

𝓡𝓡
RAVETTE PUBLISHING

Once there was a little girl,
who received a little teddy for Christmas.

She called him Teddy Christmas.

They were the best of friends for many years, and one cuddle from Teddy made the little girl fill up with love.

But one day something happened.

A small rip appeared on Teddy's chest where his heart would be.

The little girl was sad,
and wanted a new teddy.

So Teddy was taken
to the charity shop.

Teddy sat in the window for days, weeks, maybe years - but no one wanted a dusty, ripped, sad-looking bear.

So Teddy was thrown away.
It was Christmas Eve.

The end.

"Hang on!" said Teddy Christmas.
"This isn't the end!
This is only the beginning."

And he was right.

For Teddy had done a lot of thinking in the charity shop window.

He climbed down from the rubbish bin,
and looked around at the big wide world.

"Maybe there are adventures out there for me," he said. "Maybe I can make someone else fill up with love."

So Teddy Christmas followed his little button nose through the town.

As he passed the quiet shops,

he heard a strange sound:

**"SQUEAK SQUEAK SQUEAK!"**

It was a family of mice.
They were shivering and
looked very sad.

"Are you alright?"
asked Teddy Christmas.

"H...Hello," said the Mummy mouse.
"We're just very cold."

"Where is your nest?" asked Teddy.

"It's all covered in snow and we can't get in," said the Daddy mouse.

Teddy knew what to do.
He took out some stuffing from the hole where his heart would be, and gave it to the mice.

"Maybe this can help," said Teddy.

The mice were delighted. They found a nice little spot inside a shoe box and in no time at all, had made a brand new soft, cosy nest.

"Thankyou, thankyou!" said the mice,
and their hearts filled up with love.

Teddy Christmas followed his little button nose out of the town and into the countryside.

As he passed the snowy fields,
he heard a strange sound:
"BAAAH BAAAH BAAAH!"

It was a sheep.

She was shivering and looked very sad.

"Are you alright?"
asked Teddy Christmas.

"H...Hello," said the sheep.
"My wool has been sh...shorn off so the
shepherd could make a woolly scarf for
his wife's Christmas present."

Teddy knew what to do.

He took out some stuffing from the hole where his heart would be, and gave it to the sheep.

"Maybe this can help," said Teddy.

The sheep was delighted. She wrapped herself up in the stuffing and in no time at all, had a brand new soft, cosy coat.

"Thankyou, thankyou!" said the sheep, and her heart filled up with love.

Teddy Christmas followed his little button nose across the countryside and into the woods.

As he passed the icy pine trees,
he heard a strange sound:
"HO HO, OH DEAR!"

It was Father Christmas.

He was shivering and looked very sad.

"Are you alright?"
asked Teddy Christmas.

"He...Hello," said Father Christmas.
"A present fell out of my sleigh and into this holly bush, but when I tried to fetch it my beard was pulled out!"

"Now no one will believe I'm the real Father Christmas!"

Teddy knew what do.

He took out some stuffing from the hole where his heart would be, and gave it to Father Christmas.

"Maybe this can help," said Teddy.

Father Christmas was delighted.
He wrapped the stuffing around his chin
and in no time at all, had a brand new
jolly, fluffy beard.

"Thankyou, thankyou!"
said Father Christmas, but when he
looked down he saw something.

Teddy Christmas was completely empty.

He had given all his stuffing and lay on
the cold ground looking very sad.

But Father Christmas knew what to do.
He scooped up Teddy and flew all across
the land, above the forests and towns...

...until they came to a little house.

Father Christmas knocked on the door three times: "KNOCK KNOCK KNOCK!"

A little old lady answered the door. She was very surprised.

"Oh! Hello Father Christmas," said the old lady.

"A long time ago, one Christmas Eve, I brought a little girl this teddy. But one day she didn't want him any more," said Father Christmas.

"Teddy Christmas!" cried the old lady with joy, for SHE was the little girl!

"Thankyou, thankyou!" said the old lady, and her heart filled up with love.

She hugged Teddy Christmas and he was
was so happy HE filled up with love!

The little hole in his heart
was gone and he was a big, fat, fluffy
teddy bear again.

When they looked up,
Father Christmas was gone.

They went inside and had a nice cup
of cocoa and a cuddle.

Once there was a little girl,
who received a little teddy for Christmas.

She called him Teddy Christmas.

They were the best of friends,
forever...

The end.

# More books by Allan Plenderleith

### Tick which books you have on your bookshelf – complete your collection!

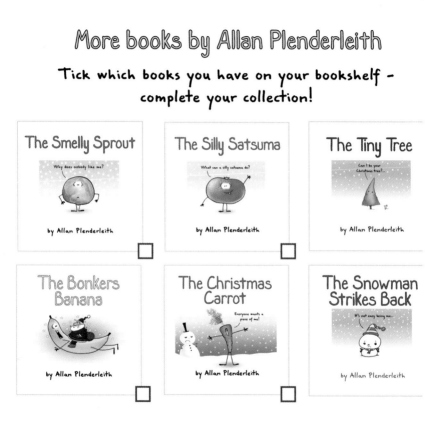

**The Smelly Sprout**

Why does nobody like me?

by Allan Plenderleith

**The Silly Satsuma**

What can a silly satsuma do?

by Allan Plenderleith

**The Tiny Tree**

Can I be your Christmas tree?...

by Allan Plenderleith

**The Bonkers Banana**

by Allan Plenderleith

**The Christmas Carrot**

Everyone wants a piece of me!

by Allan Plenderleith

**The Snowman Strikes Back**

It's not easy being me...

by Allan Plenderleith